The Pirate Pup

adapted by Bill Scollon

illustrated by the Disney Storybook Artists

Reader's
Digest
Children's Books®

New York, New York • Montréal, Québec • Bath, United Kingdom

Jake and his crew have a new friend. A playful puppy named Patch!

"Here, Patch!" yells Jake.

"Where is that silly little puppy?" asks Izzy.

Cubby offers dog treats, but Patch still doesn't come.

"Aw, coconuts!" Cubby says. "Patch always comes running when we've got treats!"

Use your spyglass to find Hook's ship, the Jolly Roger. Can you find it in the scene?

Out on the Never Sea, Captain Hook is hopping mad.
One of his boots is missing! "Barnacles!" he shouts.
Hook thinks a boot burglar is hiding on the Jolly Roger.
"Find the scurvy sea dog that took me boot!" he orders.

Hook's men look everywhere for the boot burglar.

Just as they're about to give up, Mr. Smee hears a growl.

"Well, pop me buttons," Smee says, picking up Patch. "The scurvy sea dog is a sea pup!"

Hook grabs for his boot, but Patch runs off!
Hook's men try to catch the puppy. Patch thinks
they're playing a game!
He scampers back and forth across the deck.
"Get back here you mangy mutt!" yells Captain Hook.

Find Patch in your
spyglass and on the
page. He has Hook's
boot! Do you see
the boot in your
spyglass?

Through his telescope, Jake sees Captain Hook chasing Patch!

"That puppy sure loves to play," laughs Izzy.

"Hook doesn't want to play," says Jake. "He wants to capture Patch!"

"Yay hey, no way!" shouts Izzy. "We have to rescue him!"

Look for Hook in your spyglass. What's Hook doing? Now find Patch in your spyglass.

The Never Land Pirates set sail to save Patch. Along the way, they'll collect Gold Doubloons as they solve Pirate Problems! Jake calls to his ship. "Yo ho, Bucky," he says. "Let's go!"

The Jolly Roger docks at Shipwreck Beach.
Patch races down the gangplank. Hook and his men are close behind.
"After that poppinjay pup!" Hook shouts. "I want me boot back!"

The pirates chase Patch down the beach and into the jungle.
"*Woof, woof!*" barks Patch. He's having a wonderful time!
"Follow that fur ball!" Hook says.

Does Patch still have Hook's missing boot? Look for it in your spyglass. Now find the boot in the scene.

Jake and the Never Land Pirates join the chase.
"Come on crew," says Jake. "Patch needs us!"
Patch runs deeper and deeper into the jungle.
"Shiver me timbers," says Izzy. "Where's Patch going?"

Find the butterfly on Cubby's map. Now look for it in your spyglass.

"Don't worry," says Cubby. "Patch will be okay if he takes the path on the right. That leads to Butterfly Bluff."

"What if he goes left?" asks Jake.

"That path leads to Stinkpot Swamp!" Cubby answers.

"Yuck," Izzy says, pinching her nose.

11

Patch stops at the fork in the path. Should he go left or right?

"Go right!" yells Izzy. "Go right!"

Patch listens. He turns right and scurries away.

For solving a Pirate Problem, the crew gets four Gold Doubloons!

Tell Patch to "Go right!" Then, find the Gold Doubloons in your spyglass and in the scene.

Captain Hook arrives at the fork. Which way should he go? Smee says that Izzy told Patch to turn right. "I never do as the Never Land Pirates say," the captain sneers. Hook and his men turn left!

Cubby's map was right. The left path plops the unlucky pirates right into Stinkpot Swamp! Yuck!

Search your spyglass for Hook then find him in the swamp. Next, find the butterfly in your spyglass.

But the captain is determined to get his boot back.
     He and Mr. Smee scramble out of the swamp and hurry to
Butterfly Bluff.
     Patch narrowly escapes. He jumps onto a giant butterfly and
soars into the sky!

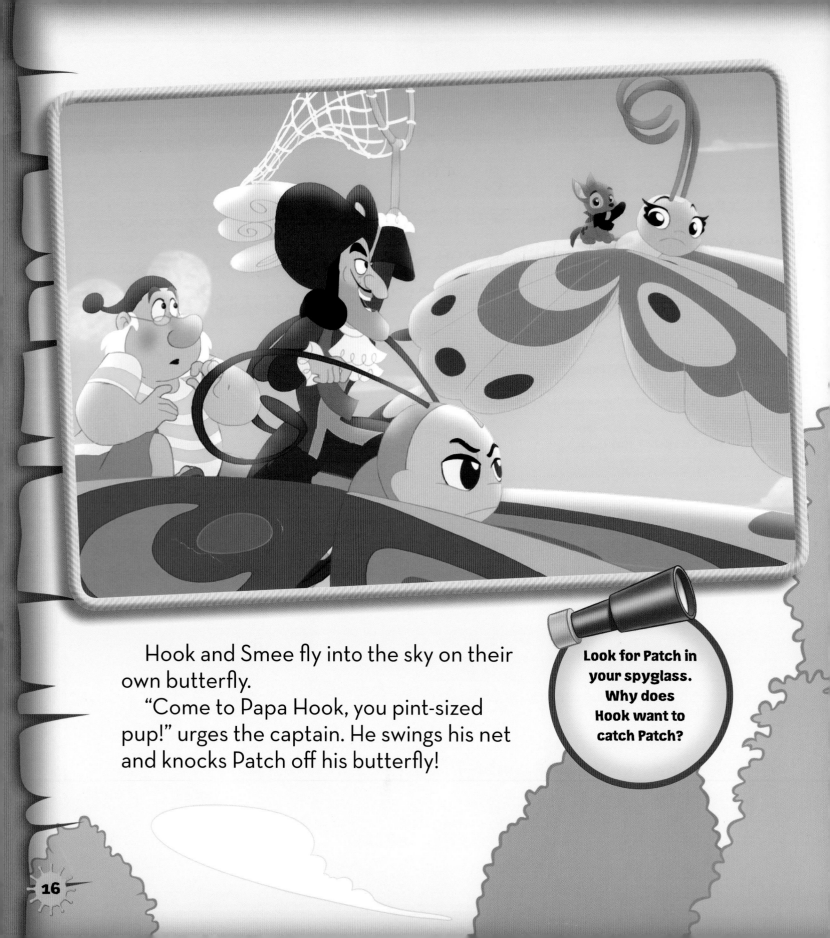

Hook and Smee fly into the sky on their own butterfly.

"Come to Papa Hook, you pint-sized pup!" urges the captain. He swings his net and knocks Patch off his butterfly!

Look for Patch in your spyglass. Why does Hook want to catch Patch?

Jake sees Patch falling toward him!
"Izzy, this is an emergency!" he cries.
"I've got it covered!" Izzy says. She quickly tosses Pixie Dust into the path of the plummeting pooch. "Pixie Dust, away!"

Count the Doubloons on the page. Can you find them in your spyglass, too?

The Pixie Dust works! The puppy floats right into Jake's arms.
"Yo ho, way to go," laughs Jake. Everyone is happy Patch is back!
For rescuing Patch, the crew collects more Gold Doubloons!

The crew returns the boot to Captain Hook. "It's about time!" he snaps.

"You could have had it sooner," says Izzy. "All you had to do was ask Patch nicely!"

Patch agrees. "*Woof, woof!*" he barks.

Do you think Hook is glad to get his boot back? Find the boot in your spyglass.

Find the Doubloons in your spyglass. How many will be added to the Team Treasure Chest?

Jake and the crew return to Pirate Island. It's time to put their Gold Doubloons into the Team Treasure Chest.

Jake cheers. "Yo ho, way to go!"

"Hey!" says Cubby. "Where's my shoe?" Patch starts to run. "*Woof, woof!*" he barks.

Izzy laughs. "Silly puppy!"